From My Tower

FEATURING CHRISTMAS AT GREYSTONE

MARGARET SELLS EMANUELSON

authorHOUSE®

AuthorHouse™
1663 Liberty Drive
Bloomington, IN 47403
www.authorhouse.com
Phone: 1-800-839-8640

Published by AuthorHouse   8/29/2012

ISBN: 978-1-4772-3206-4 (sc)
ISBN: 978-1-4772-3207-1 (hc)
ISBN: 978-1-4772-3208-8 (e)

Library of Congress Control Number: 2012912082

Books by This Author

- Lost Yesterdays
- Company of Spies, Series:
- Book I – Code-Name Jana
- Book II – Web of Spies
- Book III – New Moon Rising
- Totally Awesome – Is My Lord
- From My Tower

Foreword

It would seem to me that life is like a tall ladder, reaching from birth to the end of one's days on earth.

A young child, climbing each rung of the ladder, feels the victory that comes with a simple accomplishment. At times he will falter, perhaps fall, only to get up and try again, knowing the joy of achieving these skills and the knowledge of discovery.

As he continues to climb from rung to rung, throughout his lifetime, he will run into trials and tribulations, obstacles to overcome, avenues of discovery until at last he reaches the final rungs. Then, looking back, he can judge his growth with satisfaction or disappointment, a fulfillment or failure.

As I have grown older and pondered the existence of man, it would a seem to me that life is really a search for truth, a university of learning, reaching from Birth to the end of one's days on earth.

Learning to walk with the Lord in belief establishes in his own mind his true identity, his goals while on earth, and assures him the security of knowing his destination after he travels on to enter a new realm, a new adventure, a new University of learning – when no longer will he see through a glass darkly – but then – face to face.

And now, as I travel on to await another Commencement – a new beginning – I leave you simply a few memories of rungs of my own ladder, as I found them, jotted down on backs of envelopes, pages of textbooks, and other unexpected places.

May you find solace in the universal experience of all, and may you find them a blessing to you, as they have been to me.

Contents

Dedication

To my family: my husband Bill;
my daughters – Laura, Belford,
and our Angel – Roma;
and my sons – Beau, Jeff,
Tim, and Bruce.

And

To those who seek to Know Him.

To those who seek to Serve Him.

"For God would have all men to be
saved and come unto the knowledge of
the Truth."

Timothy II 2:6

Acknowledgments

Many thanks to those who inspired the thoughts herein.

And to Sue Gilbert, exceptional artist, who contributed her manifold talents, producing the illustration of the signature poem, *Christmas at Greystone*, and other illustrations throughout this book.

And finally, my gratitude goes to my editor, Ellen Sherwood, whose patience, careful scrutiny and advice have been invaluable.

Preface

Christmas at Greystone is the signature poem of this collection.

The following is an account of how we happened to come across its charm, buy it and reside there many years with our children.

Was it by chance? Or were we simply fulfilling the intentions of a higher power?

During the summer of 1967, a ferocious hurricane hit the East coast. The damage was extensive, and many of the beautiful homes on the Atlantic coast were demolished, to say nothing of the flooding.

But we were lucky. We had built our first house in Linkhorn Park, on a couple of acres of beautiful wooded land. It was a corner lot about two city blocks from the Princess Anne Country Club. Although Linkhorn Bay was across from us, we were protected. We had built our house there in 1946, and enjoyed the freedom and joy of our first home for many years.

It was a wonderful place to raise our five children.

That Sunday morning, after the hurricane, Bill and I were sitting in our den. He looked up from his newspaper, and said, "Looks like Andre and his brother have bought the old Masonry property. They are dividing it and putting it up for sale."

Suddenly my curiosity arose.

"Do you mean Greystone?" I was surprised. "It has a long history – and I think it was featured in the 1906 Exposition.

"You know, I have always wanted to see that house. Why don't you call him and arrange for us to go over and take a look at it?"

"Okay, I'll do that," Bill said, and immediately made the arrangements.

That afternoon, we drove into the old gates at the end of 52nd St. and wandered on down to the end where 'Greystone' sat on the shores of Crystal Lake.

I was surprised at how large it was. We pulled into the back through two large stone gates and parked.

The front of the house faced the Lake, and was surrounded by a stone wall about 3½ feet tall. The stones were carved into a design in the very front where wide steps led down to the water. It reminded me of a scene in the "Sound of Music," a movie which had come out some years earlier.

An enormous magnolia tree stood on one side of the walled garden, which reached up to the second-floor porch, adjacent to the tower. The tower was covered with Wisteria and English ivy. But we later discovered the roots of the vines had caused the tower to leak.

I was fascinated at the romanticism of the place. It was indeed what one of my German friends later called, "Peggy's 'Kline Schloss.'"

We walked around the outside. There were many windows which were open, some were cracked or broken, and the wind and rain had blown into the house, damaging the woodwork, even causing mildew in the dining room. Debris was everywhere; the entire place had felt the force and destruction of the hurricane.

We wandered around to the front of the house and entered the two double doors on the front entrance, into a large room with a fireplace at one end about 40 to 50 feet from the other side.

Across from the entrance, there were very broad steps that led up to a landing and then divided into two sides of wide steps to the second-floor Hall. At one time the area had been lit by an enormous 8-foot chandelier, but the vandals and teenagers had managed to destroy it.

The structure of the house was obviously solid, and well built. Structurally, it was completely intact.

But the atmosphere was gloomy with the dark woodwork; little light could penetrate the heavy atmosphere,

Suddenly I had a feeling of being uninvited.

We wandered around through a myriad of large rooms and halls. The house had five stories: a full basement with what must've been a rathskeller at one time; a vast first floor, with the French parlor, library, the ballroom, dining room, breakfast room, butler's pantry, kitchen and porch on the back, with an adjacent separate bedroom and bath; the second floor had multiple large bedrooms with fireplaces, a 5-foot wide hall connecting them, and a place where the elevator had once served the three main stories.

The third floor contained four enormous bedrooms, a bath and the entrance to the 4th floor walk-in attic which contains cedar closets in the storage amenities and actually could have become another usable story.

We continued to wander around, getting lost several times until finally we wound up in a room in the middle of the second floor.

We stood there for a moment, pondering our thoughts. Finally, I looked at Bill, "Let's buy this house."

He said nothing, but I could see his thoughts were churning.

Over the next few days, we discussed our options.

Everything fell into place. It was as though that house was calling us to come and restore it to its former glory. And so, we bought the house on Crystal Lake.

It was an enormous place and though we had a very large house, we needed more bedrooms.

It took us a year to restore it. Bill hired a crew who went to work painting, refurbishing, repairing and doing all the things that needed to be done.

I was now working as director of the branch office of a psychological consulting firm at that time, and so I chose to work with a particularly gifted decorator who found the materials I wanted for the window treatments, carpets, and other necessary items, one of which was to paint all of the dark walnut woodwork which had been lacquered time after time and added a gloomy atmosphere to the downstairs ballroom and dining room. He helped me choose and order the necessary amenities, including the black-and-white tile for the breakfast room, and he tiled the kitchen and butler's pantry. After a year of work and fun doing it, the house was finished. I had many antiques and other furniture in my first house, but I ordered the French furniture from Europe to be upholstered in the States for the French parlor. It was a busy year. I had always loved decorating my home, wherever I was. It was fun, exacting, to be sure, but the results were simply beautiful. We loved it.

In 1969, we moved into our new house on Crystal Lake.

That year we had a 'Castle Warming' and, to our delight, some of our friends from our old Universities, and those who lived around the lake, arrived by boat to the front steps that led down to the water

It was a wonderful time. The children could drive their boats around the lake and our youngest daughter and daredevil found that she could even go through an inlet called Rainey's Gut out all the way to Linkhorn Bay.

We settled in, worked and played together, entertained friends and enjoyed the wonders of Greystone.

And then during that following summer of 1970, the Lord came to me in a powerful way, filling my spirit to overflowing with the power of His Holy Spirit, opening our eyes to the Truth – that nothing is impossible for God.

We learned much of the ways of the Lord and His manifold Blessings.

Many incredible miracles and signs and wonders followed as we learned about the Gifts of the Spirit and how to operate in them.

The children grew up and left to finish their education and fulfill their destinies.

And so in the 1980s we left Greystone to its present owners – Frank and Juliet Reidy, who have loved and cared for it ever since.

To be sure, we shall never forget the joy of the years we were there.

Many of the insights contained in this book including *Christmas at Greystone,* came to me while we enjoyed our lives at Greystone.

May they serve as a blessing to you, as they have been to me.

Christmas at Greystone

FROM MY TOWER ROOM I SEE
HOLLY BERRIES ON THE TREE
NESTLED IN MY
GARDEN WALL,
HANGING LIKE A
CRIMSONED BANNER,
IN A MOST INTRIGUING
MANNER,
GREEN, MAJESTIC,
STRONG AND TALL,
IT IS CHRISTMAS, AFTER ALL.

SNOWFLAKES PATTER,
ONCE AGAIN,

SPLATTERING MY
WINDOWPANE,

PATTERNED PRISMS,
FRACTURED LIGHT,

ENTERTAIN MY
WONDEROUS SIGHT;

LITTLE DROPLETS
OF PERFECTION,

RAINBOWED COLORS
OF REFLECTION

TELL OF WINTER'S
PURE DELIGHT.

FIRELIGHT GLOWS FROM
YULETIDE EMBER

FROM EACH CRACKLING,
BURNING TIMBER,

WELCOMING THE
COLD DECEMBER,
WEAVING MEMORIES
TO REMEMBER;
YARNS, LONG WOVEN,
STORIES TALL,
FEATS OF HEROES'
RISE AND FALL.
IT IS CHRISTMAS, AFTER ALL.

FROM OUR KITCHEN,
OLD AND RARE,
SWEET AROMAS FILL THE AIR,
SIGNALING THE
GOODIES THERE.
JOYFUL GIGGLES
EVERYWHERE,
SNEAK WE COOKIES
WITH A FLAIR.

SINGING CHILDREN,
LARGE AND SMALL.
IT IS CHRISTMAS, AFTER ALL.

NOW WE GATHER
ROUND THE TREE,
HANGING ORNAMENTS
WITH GLEE.
MANTELS, DRAPED
WITH GREENERY,
STOCKINGS HUNG
FOR ALL TO SEE.
CANDLES LIT UPON
THE TABLE,
WEAVE AN UNEXPECTED
FABLE.
DELICACIES BY THE SCORE,
GOURMETS BECKONING
FOR MORE.

NOW WE SING A
CHRISTMAS CAROL,
AS WE "DON OUR
GAY APPAREL,"
GOWNS OF SPLENDOR
TO ADMIRE;
GENTLEMEN IN FINE ATTIRE.
RIBBONED DRESSES,
FLOWING TRESSES,
SKIP THE CHILDREN
DOWN THE HALL.
IT IS CHRISTMAS, AFTER ALL.

PREPARATIONS
NEARING CLOSURE,
PROMPT A SCURRY
AT EXPOSURE,

AS THE CLOCK BEGINS
TO CHIME,

SIGNALING ARRIVAL TIME

FOR OUR FESTIVE,
FESTOONED BALL;

HURRIED DOINGS,
TASKS ENSUING.

IT IS CHRISTMAS, AFTER ALL.

NOW THE HORSES'
HOOVES DO PATTER,

WITH A FASCINATING
CLATTER;
SLEIGH BELLS RINGING,
CAROLERS SINGING,
DOWN THE LONG
INTRIGUING MALL;
SOARING SPIRITS,
LAUGHING CHATTER,
SIGHTS OF WONDER
THAT ENTHRALL.
IT IS CHRISTMAS, AFTER ALL.

AS WE GATHER AT THE DOOR
COMES EXCITEMENT,
EVEN MORE.
SPARKLING CRYSTALS
LIGHT THE HALL;

CHERISHED FRIENDS
NOW COME TO CALL;
HUGS OF WELCOME,
JOYFUL GREETING,
LONG ANTICIPATED MEETING.

RUSTLING SOUNDS OF
SWISHING TAFFETA
MINGLE WITH THE
CHILDREN'S LAUGHTER,
PEALS OF JOY FROM
EVERY RAFTER;
GENTLEMEN, BOTH
SHORT AND TALL,
GATHER ROUND TO
START THE BALL.
IT IS CHRISTMAS, AFTER ALL.

NOW THE MUSIC
FILLS THE AIR,

WHIRLING DANCERS,
SKIRTS AFLARE,

CHILDREN, WATCHING
FROM THE STAIR,

TREASURED HOURS SLIP AWAY
AS WE DANCE
ALMOST TIL DAY.

GROUPS OF FRIENDS
AROUND THE HALL

SIP AND CHAT ABOUT
THE BALL.

IT IS CHRISTMAS, AFTER ALL.

II

FROM MY TOWER ROOM, I SEE,

IN MY STORE OF MEMORY,

HOLLY BERRIES ON THE TREE
NESTLED IN MY
GARDEN WALL,
HANGING LIKE A
GRACEFUL BANNER
IN THE MOST INTRIGUING
MANNER,
STILL, MAJESTIC,
STRONG AND TALL.
IT WAS CHRISTMAS,
AFTER ALL.

STRAINS OF MUSIC
FROM BELOW
ECHO JOYS OF LONG AGO.
RIBBONED MISSES,
STOLEN KISSES,

UNDERNEATH THE
MISTLETOE.

GUESTS ATTIRED
IN ELEGANCE

ADD ENHANCEMENT
TO THE DANCE.

HAPPY MEMORIES
LIFT THE PALL.

IT WAS CHRISTMAS,
AFTER ALL.

IN MY MIND'S EYE
I REMEMBER

LOVE THAT BLOOMED
IN THAT DECEMBER,

LIGHTED LIKE A
BURNING EMBER;

LOVERS PARTED,

BROKEN HEARTED,

LOVE THAT LASTED
THROUGH THE YEARS;

THROUGH THE JOYS AND
THROUGH THE TEARS.

SWEET ENCOUNTERS,
HANDS THAT HELD,

UNIONS, ONLY GOD
DID WELD.

IN MY DREAMS I
STILL REMEMBER

THAT ENCHANTING
COLD DECEMBER

WHEN WE LIT THE
YULETIDE EMBER

ON THAT DAY SO LONG AGO,

AND THE ONES WHO
MADE IT SO.

NOW THE YEARS
HAVE SPUN AWAY

SINCE THAT LOVELY
CHRISTMAS DAY,

STILL, THE DANCERS
BOW AND SWAY,

AS THEY WHIRL
ALMOST 'TIL DAY.

AND THE MUSIC LINGERS ON,

THOUGH OUR FRIENDS
ARE LONG SINCE GONE.

SPARKLING CRYSTALS
LIGHT THE HALL

AS THE DANCERS
START THE BALL.

IT WAS CHRISTMAS,
AFTER ALL.

III

Now I hear the joyous laughter,
ringing out from every rafter
From the ladder, strong and tall,
As *my* Children
Hang, with glee,

ornaments upon the tree
Standing in the castle's hall,
It is Christmas, after all.

Now my children take our places
And repeat the former graces,
that my family embraces,
From those season's long ago.

Now their children romp and play
Till the night has turned from day;
And the candles light the way.

And my heart is filled with love
As I watch the Holy Dove
Light upon their little heads;
As we tuck them in their beds.

Hugs and kisses, and near misses,
Pleas to stay up if they may.
They await the sun's first ray.

So we pass the message on,
As our parents did before.
What a treasured gift to store
In Our Hearts Forevermore,
Of another Christmas morn
When our Savior, Christ, was born.

Hear the Holy Spirit's call
To His children old, and small –
Jesus Beckons, Now we praise Him…
It is Christmas, after all.

The Invitation

I saw a man upon a cliff
that overlooked the sea.
And as my thoughts began to drift,
I saw Him beckoning to me.

His voice was soft, and crystal clear,
Like Music falling on my ear.
"Come nigh to me that I may part
the sorrow
From Your Aching Heart."

His arms reached out,
both strong and wide
to bring me to His

Wounded side.

His strong inviting hand
reached out,
As though I were to follow.
I, fascinated, turned to go,
The rocks were steep, then hollow.
The path lay out before my eyes,
I could not see it clearly,
And as I sought to climb the rocks,
The way grew hard and eerie.
And looking up I found that I
no longer saw him clearly.

In disappointment, my eyes searched
to reconstruct His vision;
But those I told, along the way,

just laughed in sheer derision.

I climbed beyond the doubting crowd,
I knew that He was there.
And struggling on, began to fall
in sadness and despair,

And then I heard a soft sweet voice,
"Hold on! All is not lost.
But you must learn my special ways,
And you must count the cost.

"I'll take you in my arms,"
He said, "and lift you up with Me,
Where you can see the world you left,
Beyond the restless sea.

And there you'll find

a treasure trove, no earthly
one could give;
Of peace and joy and love, My Child,
And you'll begin to live.

Then you will know you left behind
A world that's doomed to grief.

The fools who sought
the Robber's lure,
Were conquered by the thief.
The One who came to Rob and kill,
A master at deceit.

For they believed his lies And
Left the One of true belief,
And Suffer now, the consequence:

A fiery grave Beneath.

But you, my precious one,
I chose
before your seed was planted;
And from the first breath
that you drew
Your Entrance Fee Was Granted.

I knew you in your mother's womb,
Your Future choice was certain;
for I knew when you'd
come to Me
beyond the World's dark curtain.

Now, your appointed day has come,
As I Have Known It Would;

And Naught can snatch
you from My Hand,
Not Even If He Could.

"I'll take you in my arms,"
He said, "and lift you up with Me,
Where you can see the world you left,
Beyond the restless sea.

And there you'll find
A treasure trove, no earthly
one could give;
Of peace and joy and love, My Child,

And you'll begin to Live.

To Catch a Moonbeam

SOUNDS AND COLORS
REELING OFF MY THOUGHT,
LIKE TO A TIME-
OLD FISHERMAN
WHO'S CAUGHT
A MOONBEAM ON HIS LINE,
A MELODY OF STARS,
AN ENDLESS RHYME.

THE SOUNDS AND COLORS
OF MY LIFE DO MERGE:
RED, FOR THE JOY OF LIVING;

BLACKNESS, FOR THE DIRGE;

YELLOW, FOR LAUGHTER, FUN,
AND LIGHT HEART AFTER;

GREEN, FOR THE HEALING
TOUCH OF GOD'S HEREAFTER;

BLUE, FOR THE DAYS WHEN
SORROW DAMPENS DREAMS;

PURPLE FOR ROYAL
MAJESTY WHO SEEMS

ONLY TO SAY, "REMAIN
IN ME EACH DAY"

THEN WILL I MERGE THE
COLORS OF YOUR NIGHT,

INTO A PURER, BRILLIANT,
WHITER LIGHT.

MY GENTLE KNIFE WILL
SEVER BONE FROM MARROW,

AND I SHALL WIELD A TURN,
A PATH THAT'S NARROW.

I CAUSE A CHANGE OF
ACTION, BEING, THOUGHT
FOR WHICH YOU'VE
STEADFAST YEARNED
BUT FELT HAD COME
TO NAUGHT.

EVER YOU REACH, AND
TRY, AND FAIL.
DO YOU NOT KNOW I'VE
KNOWN THAT VAIL?
DO YOU NOT KNOW
I LOVE YOU YET
EVEN THOUGH GOALS
ARE YET UNMET?

SOUNDS AND COLORS REEL
NOT OFF MY THOUGHT,

MINE I HAVE KNOWN BEFORE
AND FULLY BOUGHT.

I AM THE TIME-OLD
FISHERMAN WHO'S CAUGHT
A MOONBEAM ON HIS LINE,
A MELODY OF STARS,
AN ENDLESS RHYME –

AND YOU ARE MINE.

The Dreamer

The dreams of youth,
so vainly sought,
Their wild expectancy unwrought,
Are long since dead upon their bier.

Yet passing by I shed no tear,
They were not His,
but simply mine.

Like Eagle's wings they
soared on high,
And delved the depths
of earth and sky.
Adventuring, yet then to find

The ultimate of God's design,
the universal paradigm.

And now, content to find my place,
I gladly meet Him face-to-face,
To share the wonder of His Grace.

On soaring wings, the Spirit flies,
To depths of thought
Beyond the skies,
where universal wisdom lies.

The dreams of man can ne'er succeed
Unless His sovereignty's decreed.

So thus we flounder,
unfulfilled,
Until we know what

He has willed.

So listen aptly To His Voice
Till His instructions be instilled.
Then praise lift, and hearts rejoice
That You Can Hear His
Precious Voice.

The dreams of youth,
so vainly sought,
Their wild expectancy unwrought,
Are long since dead upon their bier.

Yet passing by I shed no tear,
They were not His,
but simply mine.

Eclipse

ALAS! THE DARK THAT
CAME AT NOON
AND RUPTURED OUR
SECURE COCOON
THAT SENT ITS WAVERING
WAVES ABOUND
TO EARTH, WITHOUT
A SINGLE SOUND.

THAT RENDERED US TO
AWE AND PRAYER
TO FEEL A HIGHER
PRESENCE THERE.
AND TREMBLING SOULS
DID STOP AND THINK

"ARE WE BUT ON THAT
DREADFUL BRINK?

ARE WE PREPARED IF
COMES THE END,

OR IS OUR FUTURE
JUST PRETEND?"

AND SOME REJOICED
IN JOY AND LOVE,

WHO SAW THE POWER
FROM ABOVE,

WHO FELT THE
COMFORT OF ITS SIGN

THE UNIVERSAL PARADIGM.

A Dove to a Tower Room

From my tower room I see
Crystal prisms on the tree
Standing in my garden wall,
Green, majestic, strong and tall,
Hanging from each leafy banner
In a most intriguing manner.

Crystal prisms brightly glimmer
Set the whitened snow a-shimmer
In a miracle of ice,
Glistening, winter's paradise.

And I ponder each small prism,
Each illuminating schism,
Of His spectrums' varied rays,
Little drops of saintly praise.
Each alone a sturdy member
Of the One Divine Assembler
Who hast gathered each alone
In a rainbow, round His throne.

And my heart is filled with wonder,
Thus, considering the blunder,
When man undertakes direction,
In the light of His reflection,
From the prisms of His making.

Ah! But that we wouldst, forsaking
Idle pride, become dependent

Upon Him, Divine, resplendent,
And become a choice reflection
Of His own will and perfection;

Only then will cruelty cease
And his kingdom come in peace.

And I praise the God who made me,
And His Son who came to save me.
And I know that secret, hidden
In each prism of the rainbow –

'Tis the secret of the ages,
'Tis the Trinity, which sages
Often spoke in days of yore.
For the prisms' terse triangle
Jolts my mind's eye to untangle—

To but understand that
hidden mystery—

God the Father, God the Spirit, God,
The Son Who comes for me.

And my spirit's filled with power

As I ponder in my tower
And my tongue, unleashed in beauty,
Sings in praise and love and duty;

And my spirit flows with love
As I welcome thus the Dove,
Knowing utter sweet subjection
To miraculous perfection.

Oh! The glory that is mine
But to feel His Hand divine
Open sleeping eyes to see
Promise of eternity.

A Life-Time Of Reflection

To look beyond the
looking-glass and see
A lifetime of reflection – that is me,
Unleashed the tears that
flow but from my heart,
A heart of sorrow, broken, set apart.

A tear for every wound and every care,
A tear for every tortured deep despair.
A tear for gratitude and gentle mirth,
A tear for all the loneliness
and dearth.

A tear for every quiet unmeasured joy;
A tear for each endeavor and employ,
A tear for every precious memory,
Love that was gladly given,
and returned to me.

To look beyond my
looking-glass and see
My life's reflection
looking back at me,
Is but to search that inner secret place
In which one lives – in
honor, or disgrace.

For through a darkened
mirror, now we see
Until He, who is perfect, does appear.

Then, He, Erasing every
Image Not of Him,
Will banish every tear,
And then, a new anointing
will impart –
A powerful surge of Joy
within the heart.

To look into my looking glass and see
His changing image
looking back at me,
Is but to live in bless'ed harmony;
The past, long gone, nor
tears upon my face,
Is but to live empowered
by His Grace.

A Thorn for the Rose

I woke amidst a gentle rain
And looked out through my
Windowpane;
And there I spied a crimson rose,
Robed in majestic velvet clothes.
She turned her face towards
Heaven's blue –
And then – suddenly I knew:

I must but pluck her beauty rare.
But, breaking stem, a thorn was there,
And drawing back in wounded pain,
I saw a crimson gory stain
Flow out of me – from out my hand;

And I began to understand.

God placed a thorn <u>upon</u> His flower,
Protecting her in every hour,
To keep her perfect, untouched, pure;
To keep her from the robber's lure.
Reminded then was I of He
Who wore a <u>Crown</u> of <u>Thorns</u> for <u>Me</u>.
Each drop he shed of deepest red,
Was but a cleansing healing flow
That in the thorn He sends for <u>Me</u>
An inner beauty I may know.

God placed upon his rose a thorn
For she knows <u>Not</u> to weep or mourn;
Nor knows she anger, lust, or sin,
Nor has she unpurged fruit within.

But you and I, His treasured love,
Are shaped by power from above;
<u>Our</u> thorns are thrust <u>within</u> the flesh
That we may flower and be refreshed,
That we may ever inward grow
And produce from His aime'd bow.

Thus, let me not my thorn resent –
Knowing that it was Heaven-sent,
That might God's roses understand:
A thorn for <u>His</u> Roses
wase <u>well</u> planned.

Into His Gates

Into Your gates, Lord,
do I come,
Grateful for every battle won,
Thankful for every day of life
And every challenge
Born of strife.
For every laugh, for every tear,
For everything that one holds dear,
For every infant born at last,
For aging parents, fading fast,
For every stalwart, loyal friend,
For loved ones sharing life's brief end.

Into your gates, redeemed of blame,

Into your courts to praise Your Name,
Into Your Presence let me be,
Into close fellowship with thee.
There does a joy-filled heart to sing
Majestic wonders of my King.

Essence

TIME FLIES,
SUN RISES,
AND SHADOWS FALL.
LOVE IS FOREVER, OVER ALL.

LOVE IS GOD'S CREATION

Once I Was Blind

Once I was blind,
But now I see,
Whence came the True Reality.
And what did I discover?
Thee!

And then, did I discover –
Me.

1967

The Legend Of Glendare Castle

OLD GLENDARE CASTLE
STANDS ALONE,
AS THOUGH IT WERE AN
EARTHLY THRONE.
HIGH DOES IT SIT
UPON A HILL,
WHILE FIELDS GROW
YELLOW IN THE SUN
WITH HAPPY DANCING
DAFFODIL,
WHO CARE NOT OF
A BATTLE WON

UPON THEIR PLACE,
SO LONG AGO,
NOR OF THE ONES
WHO MADE IT SO.

IN OLDEN TIMES OF
KNIGHT AND MAID,
TWO LOVERS MET,
IT OFT IS SAID.
BUT FROM THAT
FATEFUL UNION FAIR,
THE WICKED ONE LAID
OUT HIS SNARE
AND WOVE A WEB OF
GROSS DECEIT
THAT HEARKENED
SOLDIERS TO THEIR FEET
AND MARCHED THEM ON
TO BATTLE'S BLOOD,

TIL ALL LAY DYING
IN THE MUD.

THE MAID WAS FAIR
WITH FLAXEN HAIR,

AND SHE, A DAUGHTER
OF THE KING.

HER BEAUTY NONE
COULD E'ER COMPARE.

HER KNIGHT, A
HANDSOME CAVALIERE,

ERECT AND STATELY,
STANDING THERE.

BUT JEALOUSY DID
FLY ON WING,

BY ONE WHO ENVIED
AND CONSPIRED

TO HARM THE ONES
SO DEAR ADMIRED.
AND SO, DID WEAVE A
TREACHEROUS TALE
OF LIES, AND TREASON'S
DEADLY SONG.

THE KING, CONVINCED,
DID WEEP AND WAIL,
TO THINK HIS OWN
SUCCUMBED TO WRONG;
AND SO HE SENT HIS
KNIGHT TO FIGHT,
FROM WHICH HE NEVER
COULD RETURN;
NOT KNOWING THAT HIS
KINGDOM'S MIGHT
WAS THUS DECEIVED,
AND SOON WOULD BURN.

ITS VICTIMS DRANK, A
BITTER DRAUGHT
WHEN WAS THE
PERPETRATOR CAUGHT.

WHEN IN THE FOREST
WERE THEY FOUND,
'TWAS NOT A WHISPER,
NOT A SOUND,
FOR IN SUCH BEAUTY
THEY DID LAY,
THE OLDSTERS TELL
IT TO THIS DAY.

THE TRAGIC FATE OF
KNIGHT AND MAID,
DOTH LINGER ON
THROUGHOUT THE YEARS

AND LEGENDS LINGER
AND GROW STAID
BY ALL OF PAIN'S
TORRENTIAL TEARS.

THERE IN THE MIST,
THE OLDSTERS SAY,
THE LOVERS MEET
E'EN TO THIS DAY.
THEIR SHROUDED FORMS,
BLOWN BY THE WIND,
IN EERIE LIGHT OF
NO KNOWN KEN.

AND SOME SAY WHISPERED
SOUNDS ARE HEARD,
BESPEAKING LONGING
OF THE TWO,

FROM THAT MISTY
MEETING PLACE
DO WEEPINGS
FREQUENTLY ENSUE.

FOR DOWN THE
CORRIDORS OF TIME,
ECHOES REPEAT THE
FATE OF ALL.
HENCE SORROWS COME
AND LOVE MAY GO,
BUT TIME ERASES
HUMAN WOE
FOR THOSE WHO
LIVED THEM,
NOW ARE GONE.
AND ALL THEIR
MEMORIES FADE AWAY.

BUT THOSE WHO FOLLOWED,
SANG THEIR SONG,
AND LIVED TO FIGHT
ANOTHER DAY.

THUS WISDOM'S
LEGACY IS LOST;
FOR THOSE WHO
FOLLOW, DIE IS CAST.
NOT LISTENING, THEY
PAY THE COST.
AND BLINDLY, THUS
REPEAT THE PAST.

Incense

ALAS! THE INCENSE OF THE
NIGHT DOTH WANE,
ITS FRAGRANCE NEVER
TO RETURN AGAIN,
AND THOUGH I
SEARCH TO YET
RECAPTURE AND RETAIN
ITS PRECIOUS MELODY
OF TIME,
ALAS! IT IS IN VAIN.

As One

Ah my love, my loving love –
How Happy I
That you and I
Were blessed from Heaven above –
That in His Wisdom, true, Divine,
God truly made you mine.

Behold – across these many years
Life dealt us many a blow –
To shape, to prune, with many tears
That we might really know
That we are one in every way,
In spirit, mind, and soul,
And only union with our God

Has truly made us whole.

A house divided cannot stand,
But two who yield to Him,
Together are forever one,
When'ere He dwells within.

The Dreamer

Last night, I dreamt of marbled halls,
With gilded doors and
mirrored walls,
Reflected statues, standing tall,
But when I woke – they
were not there – at all.

Envisioned nobles passing through,
With costumed ladies, two by two,
Who bowed and curtsied
at the throne.
And there was I,
yet standing all alone.

If dreams could tell
what depths do lie inside,
Reveal the past, in ways which
coincide
With hidden ventures,
travels of the mind,
Would I know more?
Who Is it that I'd find?

Would I know then,
what creature lies within?

Or is it just a farce touched fantasy
To know the depths
that dwell therein?

An Ancient Bard once said it well,
"What Fools We Mortals Be"

What Tragedy –
To never know,
One's true identity.

Behold My Heart

BEHOLD! MY HEART
REMEMBER JOY,
NOT DARKENED SOUNDS,
UNMEASURED PLOY,
DISCORDANT CLANG
OF DISTANT BELLS
THAT RANG
IN DAYS GONE BY

BUT ONLY LOVE,
AND CHERISHED LOOK,
WHEN WE
THAT CLAMOROUS
WORLD FORSOOK,

AND JOINED HAND IN HAND
TO BE AS ONE,

And from that day we trod
The path
Of work and play and aftermath,
Of children' s birth – of sheer delight
To watch them grow
Within our sight.

The tragedies and joys we've shared
Not doubting if the other cared.

I look at you and know we've won
Our victory of life –
As one.

Once We Were Young

ONCE WE WERE YOUNG –
NO THOUGHT OF
GROWING OLD,
WE SOUGHT ADVENTURE'S
ECSTASY
AND COURAGE TO BE BOLD
SEEKING THE WORLD'S
ABUNDANCE
ITS FAVOR AND ITS GOLD;
DIAMONDS OF RECOGNITION,
TO THESE OUR SOULS
WERE SOLD.
WE WANDERED THROUGH
A LIFE-SPAN,

EXPLOITED EVERY DREAM,
IGNORANT OF
ANOTHER PLAN
FOR THINGS NOT
AS THEY SEEM.
NEVER A THOUGHT
TO FATHOM
THE PRICE WE'D HAVE TO PAY.
NOR FROM A DREAM
OF LEISURE,
WE'D JOLT AWAKE ONE DAY.

THOSE WERE THE DAYS
OF SPLENDOR,
AND CASTLES BY THE SEA,
DREAMING OF DREAMS
SO TENDER
THAT NEVER E'ER COULD BE.

NOW THAT THE YEARS HAVE
TEMPERED
**THE FOOLISH ACTS
OF YOUTH,**
NOW THAT OUR HEARTS
ARE YEARNING
AND SEEKING FOR
THE TRUTH.
NOW THAT OUR THOUGHTS
ARE BURNING
FOR FREEDOM FROM
THE PAST;

WHERE DO WE FIND THAT
LEARNING
WHICH FREES A
SOUL AT LAST?

HOW DO WE FIND
DISCERNING
OR IS THE DIE NOW CAST?

WHERE ARE THE AGE-
OLD PROPHETS
WHO TOOK AWAY ALL DOUBT?
LOST IN A SEA OF SORROW
NO HOPE OF FINDING OUT?

LOOK TO THE ONE
WHO MADE YOU
HIS PRESENCE IS AT HAND
AND HE WILL GENTLY
LEAD YOU
INTO THE PROMISED LAND.

THERE YOU WILL FIND
REDEMPTION
AND SOLACE FOR YOUR SOUL.
THERE WILL YOU
SOON DISCOVER
*THAT HE HAS MADE
YOU WHOLE.*

LIVE IN THE JOY THAT
STRENGTHENS,
LIVE IN THE SON, REJOICE!
WELCOME THE
BLESSED PRESENCE
OF HIM WHO GAVE
YOU CHOICE.

REVEL IN ALL HIS GLORY,

*LIFT UP YOUR HEARTS
IN PRAYER,*

HIS IS THE WONDROUS STORY
OF HIM WHO HEALS DESPAIR.

IF YOU WILL SEEK –
HE'LL ANSWER,

IF YOU WILL KNOCK
– HE'S THERE,

CARRYING ALL
YOUR BURDENS,

FREEING YOUR HEARTS
FROM CARE.

THEN WILL YOU
SEE THE FOLLY,

THE IGNORANCE OF
YOUR YOUTH,

AND YOU WILL FIND
THE VICTORY
THAT COMES WITH HIS
BLESSED TRUTH."

Repentance

ALONE AND DESOLATE,
I STAND,

UPON THE SOFT
ERODING SAND

BENEATH MY HOUSE,
THAT I HAD BUILT

TO SEE IT SINK INTO THE SILT.

AND I CRIED OUT IN
PAIN AND GUILT,

BUT HE DID COVER
WITH HIS QUILT

OF LOVE, AND GENTLENESS,
AND THEN

BEGAN ME, TO HIMSELF,
TO TILT.

"DO COME AND SAVE
MY HOUSE",
SAID I.
"OH, NO," DID COME
HIS SWIFT REPLY.
"BUT I WILL SAVE MY
HOUSE WITHIN,
AND CLEANSE YOU FROM
YOUR GUILT AND SIN."

AND FROM THE TORRENT
OF MY TEARS,
OF SORROW, FELT AND
KNOWN FOR YEARS,

DID COME A SWIFT,
AND HOLY PEACE,
A PRECIOUS HEAVEN-
SENT RELEASE.

AND NOW I KNOW –
BECAUSE I KNOW,
THAT HE IS REALLY, TRULY
SO;

THAT HE WILL BUILD
MY HOUSE ON ROCK,
TO WHICH NO ONE CAN
MAIM OR BLOCK;

THEN I MAY START
AGAIN TO KNOW

THERE CANNOT BE
AN UNDERTOW.

NO QUICKSAND CAN
USURP MY FEET,
WHEN I, MY SAVIOR,
FULLY MEET.

The Prophet

"To where do I belong," I asked
The Font of Wisdom to unfold.
The answer came as there I basked
In Wisdom's Light of Ages Old.

"To everywhere and everything,
To wind and sky," He said to me.
"To East, to West, to North, to South,
To parts as yet unknown to thee.
Still, yet to nowhere, too," he said.
"No place where you
can lay your head.
No pillow can you call your own.
Only the place of My Abode

Can you forever call your Home."

"To WHOM do I belong?" I asked
The one in whom true wisdom basks.
"To everyone and no one known,
For these are your eternal tasks."

My power is Strong within
that moveth thee,
Into the realms of My Eternal Sea.
But for a second, you
may touch and feel,
whenever I send you to a soul to heal.
Then must I snatch you
to myself away
Perhaps To come again,
another day.

"All earthly ties to whom you cling,
I sever,
That you may know that
I AM your Forever –

I AM your Source, your Strength,
Life-giving Tree.
You are my Branch,
And You belong to Me".

One With The Wind

Why is it I sense a great and
surging flow in my inner being,
Inward glow, that lights
the day, the night,
the universe?

Is it you, my love, my own
beloved love, my life, my all?

Or is it an illusion after all?

The ebb and flow, the rise and fall.

The fleeting whisper of an
urgent call.

To live, to be – a part of
every living thing.

To merge divine with all eternity.

One with the wind, the sky, the sea.

And one with Thee.

Loneliness

THERE IS A TIME
WHEN I MAY SOW,
THERE IS A TIME
FOR REAPING,
BUT THIS I KNOW –
THAT ALL I DO
IS IN MY MASTER'S KEEPING.

IF I DIGRESS TO HIS DISTRESS,
HE LOVES ME JUST THE SAME,
FOR THIS, UPON ME
HE MAY PRESS
CONVICTION, IN HIS NAME.

REPENTANCE IS A
SACRED GIFT

FROM GOD IN
HEAVEN ABOVE;

THAT I UNFOLD MY
SINS, CONFESS,

AND SO RECEIVE HIS LOVE.

FOR ALL WHO ARE
THE SONS OF GOD

RECEIVE HIS LOVING HAND,

TO DISCIPLINE, AND
LEAD ARIGHT

FROM DOINGS THAT
ARE BANNED.

FOR LOVING MERCY
DOTH RESOUND
FROM HIS INFINITE HEART,
TO STRENGHTEN, SO
THAT I ABOUND
IN UNION – NOT APART.

ONCE KNOWING HIM –
THAT LIGHT WOULD DIM
IN LONELINESS COMPLETE
I'LL JUST EXIST,
IF I INSIST,
TO LIVE APART FROM HIM.

The Gardener

Into the garden of my heart, the
Holy Spirit enters.
He walks with me and talks with me,
His beauty to impart.
He plows the soil that dwells therein,
removing weeds and splinters,

He cultivates the soil around
the foot of every tree;
And pours his Spirit On His Own
to nurture, and set free.

The weeds then wither,
disappear,

And in the springtime season,
His young trees then begin
to flower,
Preparing gifts within each bloom,
His Spirit to empower.

For then, the Autumn Brings
His Fruit,
So plump and so inviting,
That all who seek its luscious taste
will find it thus exciting.

Then He instructs His
Treasured Ones,
Whose Gardens He Has Plowed:
"Go now and gather all my gifts
And take unto you the crowd —

To those are awaiting Me,
That they may also be endowed.

For I have chosen you, My Own,
To set the captives free,
From sin and death,
That they may be a part
of My Eternity.

"So go and gather all you will
and know that I will thus infill.
That they too may become My Flower
And seek out others, to empower.

And so, the Spirit travels on,
to seek another garden,
As yet Still Empty and Untilled,

That He May bring His Pardon.

With Breath Of Life
and Tongues Of Fire,
He Fills each Seeking Heart's
Desire,
To Know Him, as he too is Known,
Forever to Become His Own.

One Day, When Every
Garden' s found,
The Gardener's Kingdom
Will Abound
And fill his earth with
Love and Glory.

–This Is the Holy Gardener's Story.

Solitaire

ENTER MY SOLITARY WORLD,
WHERE THOUGHTS ABIDE,
WITH POWER UNFURLED.
WHERE DREAMS IGNITE
A VIVID FIRE,
TO YET FULFILL A
HEART'S DESIRE.

ENTER MY SOLITARY DREAM,
WHERE STRANGE
IMAGININGS ARE SEEN,
AND KNOW THE FLAME
OF UNLEASHED POWER,

LIKE BEAUTY OF AN
OPENING FLOWER.

ENTER MY SOLITARY
THOUGHT,

AND KNOW THE
ECSTASY WITHIN,

THOUGH I, ALONE,
CAN LET YOU IN,

WHERE SEARCHING
MARVELS, YET UNTAUGHT.

ENTER MY SOLITARY PRAYER,

THOUGH I, ALONE, CAN
BRING YOU THERE,

WHERE NOW TWO HEARTS
ARE MERGED AS ONE,

TWO THOUGHTS,
TWO DREAMS,

TWO MINDS,
ARE ONE.

ENTER MY SOLITARY WORLD,
WHERE THOUGHTS ABIDE,
WITH POWER UNFURLED,
WHERE DREAMS IGNITE
A VIVID FIRE,
TO THEN FULFILL A HEART'S
DESIRE.

My America

The Towers

On misty night, when tolls the bell,
The twins, their mournful story tell,
<u>Of evil plan and sore intent</u>
To murder young and innocent,
Who not their scheduled
time had spent,
And render thus a Nation rent.

But waked a sleeping Giant, they,
In arrogance, who chose their prey,
And foolishly considered naught
The consequence of what
they wrought.

The Giant awoke, as well he may,
And rose to fight another day.
And then with fury full unleashed
The Stealthy hid like hunted beast.
No haven do they find to hide
For All the World their deeds deride.

On darkened night,
in eerie light,
A vision of the Towers loom.
Against the sky
they stand on high
From out their unexpected tomb.
And in that night when
moon doth wane,
I see the towers once again,
Clothed in their shroud,
is heard their cry,

"We did not choose this day to die.
Lift up our flag and wave it high,
We did not choose this way to die.

Though Fate has left a crimson stain
Let not our memory slowly wane,
Nor let our blood be shed in vain,
For yet our spirits still remain
And soar beyond the earth's terrain.
Our souls cannot be torn in twain
For still our strong foundations stand,
Unshaken by the shifting sand.
Our voices send a fervent call
For freedom, not for one, but all.
Let unfurled banners lead the way,
As sacrificial blood does say,
'We've paid the price
that you may sing.

Lift up your voice –
Let freedom ring.'"

September 11, 2001

The Great Generation

We wakened in the mornings
and tidied up for school.
A mother's hug, a gentle kiss –
"Don't Break the Golden rule!"

We hurried to our homeroom
and sat down at our desk,
in dread anticipation –
"Think me we might have a test?"

Then called On to "Attention"
we prayed our father's prayer; then
put our right hands o'er our hearts –
Our Flag Was standing there.

We stood in rapt allegiance,
and spoke our pledge with pride,
for all it represented: for all
the ones who died –
for liberty and justice, –
who died to set us free.
From arrogance, unjust control,
and downright Tyranny.

We grew up in our Churches,
we knew our Lord was there, And
lifted up our voice in song,
And Praises everywhere.

We grew up with conviction –
The Word of God Was True,

And that He put restrictions
on What a man might do.

We took the path of learning
and sheer discovery,
and sought a new commencement
that made us truly free;

We honored both our parents,
but now that we were grown,
we sought to seek our futures –
now –strictly on our own.

But when that urgent call
Did come:
"Defend our liberty!"
We volunteered to go to war
to set our country free.

We went as Christians, soldiers, all,
in answer to our nation's call,

no matter what our ranks may be,
For God and Country – Liberty!

Through blood, and sweat,
and many tears,
We risked our young lives
through the years,
O'er land, in Air, and on the Sea,
we fought that evil enemy,
And finally gained the victory
To banish Satan's tyranny.

So now, we come with urgent plea
To heed this Lesson's History.

"Do not let this message go untaught,
For with our lives and
blood we fought –
and gained the freedom
that we <u>bought</u> –
The very freedoms you have sought;
Or that same Evil we defeated,
Will soon return and be repeated."

Monticello

UPON THIS BLESSED
GROUND WE STAND,

THE HOME OF ONE WHOSE
INSPIRED HAND,
IN ANSWER TO A
DESPERATE PLEA
FROM THOSE WHO
FOUGHT FOR LIBERTY,

SET FORTH AN EDICT
OF DECREE
WHICH LIBERATED
YOU AND ME.

THEIR VOICES SENT
A FERVENT CALL
FOR FREEDOM, NOT
FOR ONE, BUT ALL.
LET UNFURLED BANNERS
LEAD THE WAY
AS SACRIFICIAL
BLOOD DOES SAY,
"WE'VE PAID THE PRICE
THAT YOU MAY SING.
LIFT UP YOUR VOICE –
LET FREEDOM RING."

Wake up America!

Memorial Day
April, 2008
<u>North Beach Sun</u>

Wake up America!

Memorial Day dawns and memories of those of our ancestors and loved ones flood our hearts with love and pride.

These were the brave young lions who've fought in many wars to keep our nation free; who risked their futures and their lives to preserve the principles and tenets upon which our country was founded. God, Duty, Honor, Country was our creed.

And some of us are still "young" enough to remember the greatest cataclysm that has occurred on our planet to this day. We were there in World War II, willing to shed our blood, sweat, and tears to save a nation that we loved, and a world beyond with which we were less familiar. Had it not been for us and for our allies, the world would have been gobbled up by a madman, a self-appointed Dictator-God, who intended, ultimately, to rule the entire world.

The America we knew was the greatest nation on earth. It was so because our forefathers laid it out on the principles and tenets of a Holy God, who has protected us up until now, because as a nation we followed Him.

The very foundation of America was, and is, based on the Word of God. It is the standard which the founders of our nation embraced; upon which our Judeo-Christian laws and our moral values are based.

But today we weep, not only for our lost heroes, but for what we see happening to our beloved country.

Since World War II it seems as though an evil spirit has invaded the leadership of our "shining city on a hill," and begun to whittle away at the basic fabric of its foundations. And we are under attack not only by terrorists from without, but from within.

Persuaded by special-interest groups, global economists, and intellectual gurus, those in the judiciary have decided that individual rights supersede the rights of the "common good." The Congress has passed laws which are tearing down the morality, the belief system and the entire fabric of our nation's foundations.

Congress today reminds one of Nero, who fiddled while Rome burned. Congress can accomplish nothing, when the House and the Senate fight on every turn for political gain, and refuse to address major critical issues, wasting precious time with trivia.

"A house divided cannot stand."

America needs to get its house in order. We need unity, not division.

Our founders had the wisdom to know that only when a diversified people come into unity can there be justice for all.

It was George Washington who said, "Government is a dangerous master and a fearful servant." Another, equally wise, stated: "Power corrupts, and absolute power corrupts absolutely," was the description British Lord Baron Acton gave to government.

And we have seen corruption exposed in our leaders from the Oval Office, to the Senate, to Congress, to Wall Street, to the church, business, and everyday life.

One has only to look back in history to know that when a great civilization has allowed leadership to continue in the hands of the corrupt and morally degenerate, those who cared only for power, wealth and prestige and nothing for the welfare of the people, under their rule, their civilizations collapsed in disaster.

Even before Christ, Plato theorized the progression of governments.

In 1787, Alexander Tyler, a University of Edinburgh professor, had this to say about the fall of the Athenian Republic some 2,000 years earlier:

"A democracy is always temporary in nature; it simply cannot exist as a permanent form of government.

"A democracy will continue to exist up until the time that voters discover they can vote themselves generous gifts from the public treasury.

"From that moment on, the majority always vote for the candidates who promise the most benefits from the public treasury, with the result that every democracy will finally collapse due to loose fiscal policy, which is always followed by a dictatorship.

"The average age of the world's greatest civilizations from the beginning of history, has been about 200 years.

"During those 200 years, those nations always progressed through the following sequence:

1. From bondage to spiritual faith;
2. From spiritual faith to great courage;
3. From courage to liberty;
4. From liberty to abundance;
5. From abundance to complacency;
6. From complacency to apathy;
7. From apathy to dependence;

8. From dependence back into bondage."

As the nation's population rapidly reaches near 50% governmental dependency, the United States is now fast approaching the 'apathy' phase.

If Congress persists in bankrupting our country, even for those who do not belong here, we can say goodbye to the USA — in fewer than five years.

The Lord says: "Return to Me and I will return to you; and I will heal your land."

Wake up, America! The enemy is at the gate. Are you ready for a Dictator? It's later than you think.

II

Family Portraits

A Boggie

A BOGGIE IS A GIFT UNIQUE
WHICH MANY LITTLE
CHILDREN SEEK,
BUT SELDOM FIND,
FOR IT'S DIVINE.

A BOGGIE IS A GIFT
FROM GOD,
IT EASES EVERY PATH
YOU TROD,
THOUGH YOU MAY STUMBLE,
EVEN GRUMBLE.

A BOGGIE IS A FUNNY FACE,

AND LAUGHTER'S RING,
A WINNING RACE,
A FUN-FILLED GAME,
IT'S ALL THE SAME.

A BOGGIE IS A SPECIAL
TREASURE
FILLING DAYS WITH
LOVE AND PLEASURE.
A BOGGIE'S RARE,
BEYOND COMPARE.

A BOGGIE LIVES
WITHIN A HEART,
AND NOTHING ELSE
CAN E'ER IMPART
THE JOY IT BRINGS,
THE SONG IT SINGS.

SO, LITTLE ONE, IF
YOU SHOULD FIND
A BOGGIE, RARE, OF
THIS SAME KIND,
THEN KEEP IT CLOSELY
UNDER WRAP,
SO NONE CAN STEAL
IT WHILE YOU NAP.

SORRY, MY DEAR, YOU
CAN'T HAVE MINE,
MY BOGGIE IS A GIFT DIVINE.

TO MY OTHER MOTHER
My Aunt Margaret

To Be A Man —
To Beau

To be a man is first to be a boy,
To nestle in his mother's
arms and feel the joy
Of safe contentment, gladly met,
Secure and tender coverlet.

To be a man is, too, the interchange,
The rough and tumble years of play;
The grand surprises of
each timorous day.
The closest, yet most distant friend,

The fond exhaustion of
a summer's end.

And then – to be a man, the youth,
Armed with his cloak of
quest, his sword of truth,
Forward embarks upon
the knowledge sea,
Filled with himself –
and vague anxiety,
Searching for every answer of all time,
Knowing the "Nothingness"
he calleth "Mine."

Thus doth he ever shrivel or grow tall,
Thus doth he open mind
to hear the call.
Thus doth he open sleeping eyes to see

Ever beyond the endless boundary.

Even as once a boy he sought to trust,
Now he encompassed is with
awesome lust – Lust for the world
of True Reality,
Longing for love beyond Humanity.

Filled with desire, he seeks
the path of gain,
Yet knowing not t'would
split himself in twain.
Stumbling on, into a world unknown.
Trying to know, and feel,
and be, but shown
Utter futility; of each thus vain affair,
Finding instead, fulfillment of despair.

True, t'was a sparkling
jolt for just a season,
Yet now he knows that
ghastly fruitless reason.
Nothing he tries will fill
his heart to brim,
So in his striving all is lost within.

Reaching the end of self,
he turns to see
Into the Realm of true Reality –
And in his search of "World,"
"Adventure," "Me,"
What was his final true discovery?

To be a man is first to be a boy,

To nestle in his <u>Master's</u> arms and
feel the joy
Of safe contentment, gladly met,
Secure and tender coverlet.

To My Son: Beau

To Laura

The Vision

I see her wafting down the stair
With Glory glistening on her hair,
with graceful gestures, and an air
Of elegance, yet unaware
that all who see her tend to stare.
She draws attention everywhere.

For from the garden of her heart,
Her seeds of love do not depart
from friendships gathered
heart to heart.
And reaching out across her world,

a fellowship of joys
unfurl.
From my adore'd
little girl!

I waited for her through the year
Her Song was precious to my ear.
For even then, I knew she'd be
A treasured
Gift, from God to Me.

To Laura

To Roma

There was a girl with hair of gold
And eyes the color of the sea.
She fascinated young and old,
But in a special way for me.

For sunshine could not e'er compare
With all the flaxen of her hair.
Nor could the largest poignant bell
Toll out the depth of love to tell,
Reflect the beauty of her soul,
Her very essence yet untold.

Nor rain, nor wind, nor
pain, nor ought

Could know her battles yet unfought.
Nor know the strength
that dwells within
To overcome the quiet or din.

And yet I know, though
yet unknown,
God's light shall yet
thru her be shown
And all the joy she's meant to me,
She'll shed to all humanity.

To Roma, March 22, 1979

To Belford

TO THE GIRL WITH
THE VIOLET EYES,
I DO SURRENDER,
TO A FRIENDSHIP OF
DEEPEST HUE,
AND A LOVE AS TENDER.

LIKE THE LUSTER
OF AZURE SKY,
WITH A GRACE THAT
NONE BELIE,
AND A HEART LIKE
A BUTTERFLY;
WHO FLITS AND LIGHTS

ON A GLOOMY DAY,
AND GIVES COMMAND
IN A LAUGHING "STAY"
TO CHASE MY DREARY
CARES AWAY.

TO THE GIRL WITH
THE VIOLET EYES,
HER GRACE AND SPLENDOR,
TO A LOVE OF THE
DEEPEST HUE,
I DO SURRENDER.

TO BELFORD

To Jeff

Baby fingers baby toes –
what a miracle! – Goodness knows!

How you loved my rocking chair,
as I sang you into sleep.
Hoping it would always last,
HYMNS I learned so long ago,
repetitions of the past.

Playing games, with mischief's plan,
"Now, You Catch Me If You Can!"
What a darling 'Little Man.'

Medals won in swimming feats.

Gymnastics conquered
in school meets.
Surfing waves upon the sea,
higher than the tallest tree.

Racing Cars, and Flying Planes,
High above God's Earth's terrains.

Building bridges, friendships deep,
precious memories to keep.

Yet through all your life
you've known,
that you truly are God's own.
May he bless my little boy
who has brought us such great joy.

To Jeff

To Special Friends

Intelligens

Intelligens, how cruel
thou art!
Thou willst not come, for me, apart.
How happy I, a child of three, when
Good King Watson ruled o'er me,
And I Could Simply Mindless Be.
Now thou returnst to torment me.

If you will not yield to my direction,
I will resort to insurrection –
and
I will take away thy 'G'
and what will thou be
without thy 'G,'
Intelligens?

To Virgil Ward

A Hyacinth For Angie

Delicate fragrance wafts upon
the air,
Just to remind us –
Angie is still there.

Violet azure –
windows of her soul—
Still light our days,
our nights,
As the bells toll.

Yet in her poignant velvet majesty,

She let me know her precious destiny;
Just as the bell shaped
blossom of her flower
Spoke to me deftly in her final hour –

"See me? I am her violet
perfumed bell –
Tolling the joys of future life to tell."
She is now crossing o'er the boundary
Into God's vast divine eternity.
Angels rejoice, and I but chime in key,
As they proclaim
Her Final Victory.

TO ESTHER

The Cookie Monster

came today,
Alas to my complete dismay
Petite and beautiful was she
No Monster she could ever be,

T'was but her cookies, sweet and rare,
her baking skills, beyond compare,
That earned that name
and thus her fame.

Yet! Oh to my complete surprise
Those cookies led to my demise!
I cannot get up off my couch!
I have become

a dreadful slouch.

I am completely adipose

Skirt closures come not even close!

So, Friend, do take my sound advice,

If Monster Cookie Comes Your Way,
welcome the Baker without delay

For she is precious, lovely, nice,

But not her Monster Cookies, Pray!

For soon you'll find yourself addicted,

As this silly poem's predicted!

To Peggy, the Cookie Monster

Christmas Love, from Margaret

Ode To Anthony

To Anthony, our sainted bard,
We lift our glasses with a cheer
For lifting us when life is hard
His voice so sweet in song, so dear,
That birds do stop and fly around
To find that precious tinkling sound.

Though manor born and
manner gracious,
A touch mischievous and audacious,
Deft raconteur with hearty laughter,
lifts our spirits to the rafter.
Remembering for just a while
old thoughts provoke a loving smile,

for those we've loved can still impart

that joyous song within a heart.

So, lift your glasses with a cheer
To Anthony, our sainted bard
For lifting us when life is hard.
His voice so sweet in song, so dear,
That birds do stop and fly around
To find that precious tinkling sound

From Margaret

Ode To The Dabney

He dabbles here, he dabbles there,
He dabbles almost everywhere.
His genius bold,
We oft are told,
So lofty none can e'er compare.

As "Jack of trades" he oft is known,
Par excellence his deeds are sown.
His stately charm
Can cause alarm
When youngish maidens
flock around.
But take no heed,
in this young steed

The heart of chivalry is found.

So raise a cheer for our "Old Dear,"
In tribute lift your glasses high,
And praises great, your voices sing –
A little Dab's a wondrous thing.

If you should find a Dabney, free,
Please nab and hold him just for me.

From
The Margaret (the poet)

Dabble = experiments, to try
your hand at; dip into; explore

To Joey

Besides – Friend's may come
and friends may go

But there is one thing that I know,

"Chicken Friends are best, You know!!

Love from, Margaret

My Angel

She rushes here, she rushes there,
She rushes almost everywhere.
A ministering Angel, she,
Caring for Family – all three,
And now – for me!
Never a murmur, or complaint,
She Is Indeed a Treasured Saint!!

The Lord once said –
"Now be aware,–
My Angels appear most anywhere."
So if you're needing help, my friend,
Just Ask the Lord quickly to send
One of His Angels to assist.

It Is a Gift you'll not resist.

Sorry, my dear, you can't have mine!
My Angel is a gift Divine!

Thank You

How do I say "Thank You?"
Let me count the ways.

Shall I ask for sunshine to
brighten up your days?

Or just a sweet contentment
to permeate your being,

Perhaps a new anointing – a
special way of seeing?

Do I ask for gifts from God to
guide you on your travel?

And that problem's constant
worries, God will soon unravel?

Do I ask the gift of joy that you
may thus be strengthened?

And your days be filled with fruit,
and all of them be lengthened?

Or that you reap that keen delight
you give when you are giving

All those thoughtful things you do
which make a life worth living?

Yet, of all the many things
that I might ask for you

Is that God's Love will find you
in whatever you may do.

May your friendships blossom,
may your trials be few.

How else am I to find a way to
tell my friend: "Thank You?"

From Margaret

The End

"This Is Not the End,
This Is Not Even the
Beginning of the End,
But It Is the End
Of the Beginning."

Winston Churchill

About the Author

Dr. Margaret Emanuelson is a clinical forensic psychologist and a veteran of the O.S.S., America's first Central Intelligence Agency.

- The author of the series, "*Company of Spies:*" Book 1 *Code Name Jana*; Book II, *Web of Spies*, Book III, *New Moon Rising*; and the following inspirational books: *Totally Awesome*; *Lost Yesterdays*, and *From My Tower*, she has been a columnist for the "North Beach Sun," and has written for several periodicals.
- Her speaking engagements

include the American Medical Association Symposium on Medicine and Religion, and a radio series: "God's Psychology."

An Anglican Catholic and member of the Order of St. Luke, the Physician, she resides with her husband in Scottsville, Virginia.